ANDREW KAUFMAN was born in the town of Wingham Ontario. This is the same town that Alice Munro was born in, which makes him the second best writer from a town of three thousand. He also writes for film and television. He lives in Toronto with his awesome wife and their two children.

By the same author

All My Friends are Superheroes
The Waterproof Diaries
Born Weird

ANDREW KAUFMAN

The Tiny Wife

Illustrated by Tom Percival

The Friday Project
An imprint of HarperCollins*Publishers*
77–85 Fulham Palace Road
Hammersmith, London W6 8JB
www.thefridayproject.co.uk
www.harpercollins.co.uk

This edition published by The Friday Project 2013

1

First published in hardback by The Friday Project in 2011

A catalogue record for this book
is available from the British Library

ISBN 978-0-00-743923-2

Typeset in Adobe Caslon by G&M Designs Limited,
Raunds, Northamptonshire
Printed and bound in Great Britain by
Clays Ltd, St Ives plc

For the extremely patient,
and exceedingly tall, Marlo

BOOK ONE

BOOK ONE

1.

The robbery was not without consequences. The consequences were the point of the robbery. It was never about money. The thief didn't even ask for any. That it happened in a bank was incidental. It could have just as easily happened in a train station or a high school or the Musée d'Orsay. It has in the past and it will in the future, and shortly after 3 p.m. on Wednesday 21st February it happened inside Branch #117 of the British Bank of North America.

The bank was located at the corner of Christie and Dupont in downtown Toronto, Ontario, Canada. There were thirteen people inside when the thief entered: two tellers, the assistant manager, and ten customers waiting in line. The thief wore a flamboyant purple hat and brandished a handgun. Having a flair for drama, he fired a single shot into the ceiling. Bits of plaster fell from the it got caught in the fake fur fibers of his hat. Everyone was quiet. Nobody moved.

'While this is a robbery …' the thief said. His accent was thick and British, the kind that makes North Americans feel slightly ashamed. He flicked his head and a cloud of plaster dust swept into the air. 'I demand only one thing from each of you and it is this: the item currently in your possession which holds the most sentimental value.'

With a wave of his gun the thief directed the bank personnel to come around the counter and get into the line where the customers waited. At the front of this line stood David Bishop, a penguinesque man of forty-five, who trembled slightly as the thief came so close that the brim of his purple hat brushed against David's bangs.

'Well?' asked the thief.

David reached inside his jacket, removed his wallet, and pulled out several hundred dollars.

'You expect me to believe that money is the object currently in your possession holding the most sentimental value?'

David Bishop became confused. He continued to hold the bills high in the air. The thief placed his gun against the man's left temple.

'What is your name?' the thief demanded.

'David. David Bishop.'

'David David Bishop, rip the money into little pieces and throw the pieces into the air.'

Pausing briefly, David did as the thief demanded. Pieces of money fell to the floor.

'Now, David, think. You have a lot riding on this. What is the most significant, memory-laden, gushingly senti-mental object currently in your possession?'

David Bishop pointed to a cheap-looking watch on his wrist.

'Convince me.'

'My mother gave it to me – years ago, when I left for university. I've just gotten it fixed and started wearing it again.'

'Now that's more like it!' the thief exclaimed. He took his gun from David Bishop's head and the watch from his wrist. 'Now go over there and lie on the floor.'

David Bishop complied.

With a wave of his gun the thief directed the next person in line to step forward. Her name was Jenna Jacob.

In her right hand were two diamond earrings. She put these in her pocket, searched through her purse, and removed two wrinkled photographs.

'Very cute,' the thief said. 'How old?'

'Ten and thirteen.'

'You will never be more aware of how much you love them than right now.'

Jenna Jacob nodded and, without being asked, joined David Bishop face down on the floor.

My wife was next in line. I wasn't there, of course, but she told me this story so many times, told me all these stories so many times, and with such rich and inclusive detail, that I not only feel as if I was there, but I've even begun to believe it. I remember how Stacey straightened her posture before stepping forward.

'You look so much like my brother,' she said. This was true. The thief had the same crook at the bridge of his nose, and pale blue eyes that spoke of both arrogance and desperation.

'Sorry, but that doesn't exempt you.'

'You know, you don't have to do this.'

'Maybe. But, more likely, I do.'

'Why?'

'You'll see.'

'Does it make you happy?'

'It gives me meaning.'

My wife nodded and then fished around in her purse and pulled out a calculator.

'I was using this in my second-year *Calculus of Several Variables* class when the man who'd become my husband sat down beside me. I used it to help him with his homework. Much later I used it to figure out the night we got pregnant, and the day I'd give birth. I used it to calculate our mortgage and whether we could afford a second car or a second kid. There has not been an important decision in my life that I've made without it,' she said.

All these things were true. That calculator really was the object that held the most emotional significance for her. It went beyond the things she figured out with it – my wife loved math. It made sense to her. It made the world make sense to her.

She sighed deeply as she put the calculator in the thief's outstretched hand. 'Any way I can get it back?' she asked.

'I'm afraid not. How long?'

'I got it in first year.'

'No, your husband.'

'Seven years.'

'And you still love him?'

'I think so.'

'Kids?'

'Just one.'

The thief nodded. He waved his gun, and Stacey joined the others lying face down on the floor.

The thief worked through the rest of the line. Daniel James gave him his wife's parents' wedding photo, which he'd been taking to get restored. Jennifer Layone gave him a dog-eared copy of *The Stranger* by Albert Camus. Sam Livingstone, the assistant manager, who'd stood last in line, handed over the paystub from his recent promotion.

When he'd collected an item from everyone in the room, the thief backed toward the door. At the exit, he paused.

'Ladies and gentlemen, your attention please,' he said. No one got up, but everyone raised his or her head. 'It has come to my attention that the vast majority of you, if you even believe you have a soul, believe it sits inside you like a brick of gold.

'But I'm here to tell you that nothing could be further from the truth. Your soul is a living, breathing, organic thing. No different than your heart or your legs. And just like your heart keeps your blood oxygenated and your legs keep you moving around, your soul gives you the ability to do amazing, beautiful things.

'But it's a strange machine, constantly needing to be rejuvenated. Normally, this happens simply by the doing of these things, like a car battery recharging by driving.'

The thief stopped, put his arm into his sleeve, and sneezed. 'Excuse me,' he said. He looked at his watch. 'I'm really using a lot of metaphors today. Listen, I'm in a bit of a rush, so let me conclude. When I leave here, I will be taking 51 percent of your souls with me. This will have strange and bizarre consequences in your lives. But more importantly, and I mean this quite literally, learn how to grow them back, or you will die.'

The bank was quiet. The thief threw his hat into the air and was through the doors before it landed on the floor.

2.

The first manifestation began six hours later for Timothy Blaker, who'd stood seventh in line, four behind my wife. He was twenty-seven years old and worked as a bus driver. The object he had given the thief was an engagement ring, one he happened to have been eager to get rid of. He'd been carrying the ring for seventeen months, since the night Nancy Templeman, his girlfriend of two and a half years, had refused to accept it.

Timothy had not seen her or talked with her since the night of his failed proposal, so when he opened the doors two stops east of Shaw on College and she stepped inside, he was surprised to see her. Nancy extended her hand but did not deposit change – instead, she reached into his chest and pulled out his heart. She held it in front of him. He watched it beat. The bus continued to idle as he watched her run back down the steps and into a waiting yellow Ford Mustang.

Nancy stepped on the gas, the back tires producing much sound and smoke. Timothy Blaker gave chase.

The bus did not corner as well as the muscle car, but, having no heart, Timothy drove fearlessly and managed to stay on her tail. The passengers stayed in their seats, watching with fear as all their stops went by. They were underneath the Gardner Expressway, heading east on Lakeshore, when he pulled up beside her. They raced neck and neck. They ran many red lights, but at Lawrence Street cement trucks gridlocked the intersection and they were forced to stop. Many of the passengers stood, alarmed, but their fear remained too great for any of them to venture toward the front of the bus.

Timothy opened the doors. The cement trucks cleared the intersection. The light turned green and he jumped, landing with a metallic thud on the hood of the Mustang.

Timothy looked through the windshield. He could see his heart on the passenger seat. He watched it beat. He saw her jerk the steering wheel to the left and the right. He felt himself get thrown violently around. The tips of his fingers ached, but he held tighter and tighter, and then she slammed on the brakes.

Timothy was thrown from the hood of the car and landed on the asphalt. Three backward somersaults later he came to a stop.

He was bleeding from his elbow. There was a large cut just below his eye. He jumped up and a sickening pain went through his right leg. The Mustang was three hundred feet away and pointed toward him. He looked at

Nancy. She looked at him. He heard the engine rev. The back tires squealed.

Timothy did not move. The yellow 1964 Mustang sped forward. It was a hundred meters away, and then it was fifty, and then it was twenty. He did not move or shut his eyes. He stood there, watching it approach. This standing, this not flinching, made him feel strong. The closer the car came, the greater danger he was in, the stronger not flinching made him feel. It came closer and closer. Timothy continued to stand his ground and, with less than ten feet between him and the front bumper of the Mustang, she again hit the brakes. The car stopped with sudden force. His heart was thrown from the passenger seat. It burst through the windshield, leaving a heart-shaped hole in the glass, and flew directly into his chest.

3.

Three days after the robbery, and merely minutes after we'd finally gotten Jasper to sleep, our phone rang. It was our home line, which we usually let go to voicemail, but Stacey raced to answer it. Later she would explain that it had sounded urgent – an alarm, not just a ring.

The caller was Detective William Phillips, who had stood ninth in line and had given the robber a large antique key. Detective Phillips asked if anything peculiar was happening in her life, anything new and, perhaps, inexplicable. She asked him to elaborate. The detective told her that in the last twenty-four hours he had received confessions from two different husbands, claiming to have murdered their wives. He went on to explain that both of these cases involved someone who'd been inside Branch #117 at the time of its robbery.

Stacey asked for still more detail. Detective Phillips related the following stories.

* * *

Two mornings after the robbery, Daniel James, who had stood fifth in line and had given the thief a photograph of his wife's parents' wedding was tying his shoes when the lace in his right shoe broke. He put on his other pair of dark shoes and the lace in the left shoe broke. He changed into his light suit but, when tightening the lace on his right brown shoe, it, too, broke. He looked at the lace in his hand. He looked at the laces on the floor. 'I have to leave you,' he said to his wife, but she was already gone.

* * *

That same day Jenna Jacob woke to discover that she was made of candy, an event she remained unaware of until she was in the shower and looked down and saw a white film swirling to the drain.

Shocked and disbelieving, Jenna turned off the tap and wiped the steam from the mirror. Her skin was made of white sugar with mint speckles. Her hair was licorice. Her eyes were caramels. The longer she stared at her reflection, the less strange this candied version of herself became. She wrapped a scarf around her licorice hair, put sunglasses over her caramel eyes, and went downstairs. Her sons, aged ten and thirteen, barely noticed.

When her kids wouldn't eat their breakfast, she rubbed her hands together over their cereal bowls, dusting their Shreddies with sugar. When they wouldn't get

dressed and into the car, she broke
off her pinkie fingers and used
them as bribes. When she
dropped them off at
school, they were
unusually eager to kiss
her goodbye.

Jenna returned home,
called in sick, and spent the
day watching television. Just
after nine, her husband came
home.

'Sorry I'm so late,' he said.
'It's the Meyer's account
again. Why's it so dark
in here? Is there
anything to eat?'

Jenna patted the
cushion beside
her. Her husband
sat down. He
kissed her candied lips.
He kissed her neck and her
arms and her face. They went upstairs.
He kissed every part of her body.

'I could eat you up,' he said,
and, lost in passion, he did.

* * *

'Are you joking with me?' I heard my wife ask.

'Unfortunately, I'm not. I've found several other cases. One in Halifax, three in the southern United States, also in Lille, France, Barcelona, and Winnipeg. It's the same m.o. – purple hat, emotionally significant object, the whole thing. You are in danger.'

'Am I?'

'There will be a meeting of all the survivors, everyone who was inside Branch #117, this Monday at 7.15 at St Matthew's United Church. I can't stress enough how important it is that you attend.'

'Well, thank you for your call,' my wife said. She hung up, but her hand remained on the phone.

4.

That night I was in the bathroom brushing my teeth when Stacey called for me, and her voice held such urgency that I carried my toothbrush into the bedroom. She stood in front of the mirror, staring at the neckline of the T-shirt she most often wore to bed. She pointed out how baggy it was, which I hadn't noticed – the neckline plunged, and now cleavage was showing.

'Nothing wrong with that,' I said. I held her from behind. I tried to kiss her neck. She twisted away from me.

'I'm shrinking.'

'You're not shrinking.'

'You need to listen to me.'

'Couldn't it just be the laundry?'

'Even inside, I can feel it. I'm shrinking.'

'That guy's just put this into your head and you've run with it. You know how you're prone to run with things.'

'For once can you not question everything I say?' Stacey asked.

I sat down on the bed. There was a tape measure on the bedside table, unmoved from some renovations we'd been contemplating. I picked it up with my free hand.

'Why don't we measure you?'

'I don't know how tall I was before.'

'It'll be on your driver's license.'

'Right,' Stacey said. She ran downstairs and returned with her driver's license and a pencil. I put my toothbrush down where the tape measure had been sitting. Making sure her knees were straight against the doorframe, I patted her hair down and stroked a black line on the white paint of the wall. We opened the tape measure.

'One hundred and fifty-nine centimeters.'

'Oh my God.'

Stacey handed me her license. Her height was listed as one hundred and sixty centimeters.

'They could have made a mistake,' I said. 'Or maybe we should measure again?'

I stood by the door. I measured again. Her exact height was one hundred and fifty-nine centimeters and one millimeter. I read the license again. It still said that she should be one hundred and sixty centimeters tall. Stacey continued to sit on the bed, staring at the wall.

5.

In the morning we measured her again. She put her heels against the door jamb and straightened her posture. I pushed down her hair and made sure the pencil was flat. A second black line was made on the white paint. She stepped forward and I measured.

I decided to be as precise as I could be. I measured to the millimeter. What I found was not good. Yesterday she stood 1,591 millimeters tall; now she was 1,581 millimeters, a loss of 10 millimeters overnight and 19 millimeters in total.

We sat on the edge of the bed. Her feet didn't touch the floor. I couldn't remember if they ever had. I turned the tape measure in my hand. Stacey watched the floor and I watched her.

The rest of the day was spent measuring things. Stacey and I became obsessed with it. We measured the length of our bed, and the distance between the bedspread and the floor, and how far apart the curtains were when open. We measured our incisor teeth and the circumferences of our necks. We went outside and calculated the combined length of the cracks in the sidewalk in front of our house, and the average amount left unsmoked on discarded cigarette butts. We measured all that. We measured the next day too, and then we picked up Jasper from daycare and drove straight to St Matthew's United Church. I parked across the street. Jasper started crying.

'I guess I'd better go,' Stacey said. I measured the concern in her voice and agreed.

Stacey leaned between the seats and kissed Jasper. This made him stop crying momentarily, but he started again when she got out. She shuffled over the curb and up the stairs of the church. The arms of her sweater and the cuffs of her pants were turned up several times. She looked back twice, both times at Jasper.

The account of what followed is what Stacey told me happened. I have no reason to doubt that she told me anything but the truth, but I admit that I did not witness any of these events. Stacey told me that her initial impression was that the basement of St Matthew's United Church had been chosen because the dingy linoleum floor, low ceiling, and florescent lighting made it the perfect place for a support group to meet. Folding chairs had been unfolded and placed in a circle. A stack of upturned Styrofoam cups sat beside a giant silver pot of drip-brewed coffee. The only thing missing was everybody else: Stacey had arrived exactly on time, but even Detective Phillips was nowhere to be seen.

Stacey filled a white Styrofoam cup and stirred in sugar with a brown plastic stick. To the right of the coffee pot were a fan of name tags and several Sharpie magic markers. Stacey uncapped a marker, but as the tip touched the paper she paused. An inkblot formed on the top left corner of the name tag. When she started writing again, she did not write *Stacey*; she wrote *Calculator*. As she placed the sticker on her chest, she heard someone coming down the stairs.

The steps were heavy and quick and belonged to a woman. When she reached the bottom of the stairs she did not stop to introduce herself. She took the folding chair from the top of the circle and dragged it across the floor to the west wall, where a small window near the top looked onto the street. She stood on the chair and stared out the window. Several other sets of footsteps went by, and then she breathed. She jumped off the chair and joined Stacey by the coffee.

Stacey pretended to focus on her name tag so she could study the woman without looking directly at her. Her clothes were wrinkled, ripped, and dirty. She looked very tired and smelled of stale sweat. It took several moments before Stacey recognized her as the woman who'd stood four behind her, who'd handed an opened envelope, the kind you'd send a letter in, to the thief. The thief had taken it without question.

She looked at Stacey's chest, uncapped a marker, and wrote *Envelope* on a name tag. She put it on. 'Where is everybody?' she asked.

'Beats me,' Stacey said

They sat next to each other in the circle of unfolded folding chairs. Ten minutes passed, and then Detective Phillips came down the stairs. He smelled of cigarettes. Seeing their name tags, he stepped to the table, wrote *Front Door Key*, and placed it on his chest. He poured a coffee and joined them.

Next down the steps was Jennifer Layone, then Sandra Morrison and finally Grace Gainsfield. David Bishop came in five minutes later, and then Diane Wagner five minutes after that. The seven of them sat in a circle among the thirteen chairs. They waited another fifteen minutes. No one spoke and they all looked at the floor.

'I guess …' Detective Phillips said, 'we should start?'

'Could I?' Jennifer Layone asked.

Everyone looked up from the floor and directly at her. She was in her mid-twenties, wore thick-framed black glasses, and had shoulder-length blonde hair. Her skirt was long and ruffled and her boots were second-hand.

'This is gonna sound very, very strange,' she said.

* * *

On Thursday 22nd February, one day after the robbery, Jennifer Layone was searching underneath the couch for the remote control when she found God. He looked almost exactly like she'd expected him to look – long white beard, robe, sandals, the whole thing. But he was very dirty. It was dusty underneath her couch, and since she was doing laundry anyway, she took him with her to the laundromat.

Jennifer put him in a washing machine. She was running low on quarters, so she washed him with a load of jeans. She must have forgotten to check the pockets because when she took God out of the washing machine, he was covered with little bits of Kleenex. This disappointed God. He wouldn't look Jennifer in the eyes and he left the laundromat without saying goodbye. Now she was no closer to God than she'd been before the robbery.

* * *

Jennifer Layone concluded her story and everyone was silent. At the back of the room was a radiator, which clicked.

'The thing is,' Jennifer continued, 'ever since that moment I've been looking for him. Not all the time, but with whatever else I'm doing, whether I'm at work or downtown, I'm looking for him. I honestly expect to see him sitting at the back of the bus, or between files in the file cabinet, or in the refrigerator behind the milk. And even though he never is, that's enough for me. It's all I need.'

Jennifer looked down at her hands. The clicking of the radiator continued. The woman who'd written *Envelope* on her name tag stood up. Her folding chair slid backward and fell over. 'That's it?' she yelled. 'That's all that happened to you?'

Then, as quickly as she started, she ceased to speak. She froze and looked toward the stairs. Everyone turned to see what she was looking at, and it was at this moment that a lion ran down the stairs and into the basement.

The lion stopped in front of the table where the coffee was. It licked its black lips with its pink tongue. It sniffed the air, turned, looked directly at the woman whose name tag read *Envelope*, and leaped toward her.

* * *

Three days after the robbery and three months and five days after she'd left her boyfriend of six years, Dawn Michaels was walking across the living room of her newly rented apartment when she felt a searing pain at the bottom of her leg. She doubled over and clutched her calf with both hands. She rolled on the ground. The pain was unlike anything she had ever felt before, and it caused her to scream. She kept her hands around her calf and her eyes closed. The pain was coming from the lion tattoo just above her ankle. Dawn had gotten the tattoo almost exactly three months earlier.

It had been a way to commemorate the newly discovered courage that had allowed her to leave her boyfriend. It had just finished healing completely. Blood soaked into her sock and then the tattoo leaped off her skin.

Its smell was musky, and for a moment she remembered a circus her grandmother had taken her to when she was six. The lion's eyes were dark and its slit-shaped pupils were frightening. It wasn't colored the green and gold of her tattoo, but in true-to-life yellows and oranges and black. It grew and grew until it was full-sized. The lion stood in front of her, its mane moving with the breeze coming in the living room window. Dawn could feel its sour breath on her face. The lion narrowed its eyes. It came nearer. Dawn turned and ran. She ran as fast as she could and the lion chased her. Neither had stopped moving since.

* * *

'This way,' Stacey yelled. They ran through the circle of chairs, and through a door at the back that led to a large hospital-sized kitchen. Stacey shut the door and put her weight against it. The lion charged and the door kicked but she managed to keep it closed.

'Over there,' Stacey said. She nodded toward a back door at the far end of the kitchen and continued to keep both her hands and all her weight against the door. 'What's your name?'

'Dawn.'

'I'm Stacey.'

The lion's right paw came through the gap between the door and the frame, claws extended.

'You need to run now, Dawn,' Stacey said.

Dawn ran. The lion crashed into the door and knocked Stacey to the ground. It growled as it leaped through the kitchen. Ignoring Stacey completely, it raced out of the church. Stacey stood up. She ran a hand over her clothes and walked back to the meeting room.

'Should we ...' Detective Phillips started. He paused.

'Let's meet again,' Stacey suggested. 'How's tomorrow?'

Those in attendance nodded vigorously.

6.

Not everyone inside Branch #117 at the time of the robbery met a bitter or tragic end. There were several cases in which the manifestations were neither devastating nor crushing. Where, in the end, little changed. Such was the case of Sam Livingstone, who had recently been promoted to assistant manager in the bank. Although he had taken the afternoon of the robbery off, he'd gone back to work the next day.

Sam sat twirling clockwise in his chair. He did not know why he'd been promoted. He didn't feel he deserved it. Ever since he'd received the promotion he'd sat in his new chair, behind his new desk, in his new office, completely unable to get anything done. Sam shut his eyes and imagined he was underwater. When he opened them, he was. Everything was underwater. Exactly the same, just underwater. His phone rang. He picked up the receiver and noticed how much lighter it felt.

'Sam Livingstone,' Sam said.

'Sam?' asked Tim. Tim and Sam were promoted at the
same time. 'This is gonna sound—'

'My office is underwater too.'

'Really?'

'Yeah.'

'What are we supposed to do?'

Something crashed into Sam's office door. 'Hold on,' he said. 'I gotta call you back.'

Sam leaped from the chair, swam over his desk, and unlocked the door. Sam's new boss bobbed in the hallway.

'Why was this door locked?'

'I needed to concentrate.'

'I see,' she said. 'What are you working on?'

'The Barkhouse matter.'

'The Barkhouse matter? I thought you were on Samuelson.'

'Nope, still Barkhouse.'

'I need that done.'

'Finishing it now.'

Sam's boss nodded, swiveled on the carpet, and swam down the hall. Sam looked at his watch. It was 11.30 a.m. After lunch Sam realized he could float. He floated up to the ceiling. It was fantastic; it felt like flying.

Sam swam out of his office. He did a long, graceful somersault from the ceiling down to the photocopier and then back up to the ceiling. The tellers pretended not to see him.

Around 3.30 p.m. Sam swam back into his office. He locked his door and sat down in his chair. An hour later he'd finished the Barkhouse matter and emailed it off to his boss.

Just after he hit 'send' Sam kicked something under his desk. He looked down and, for the first time, noticed a big plug stuck in the floor. Being curious, he pulled on it. The plug didn't budge. He grabbed it with both hands and pulled again. The plug came free and Sam fell back into his chair. The water started draining. In ten minutes, all the water was gone.

* * *

Nine days after the robbery, while sitting alone at a table for two in a crowded restaurant, Sandra Morrison became convinced that her heart was a bomb that would go off in ten minutes. She knew the notion was ludicrous, yet her palms began to sweat and her cheeks flushed. Her heart beat faster, which made her worry all the more.

Sandra checked her watch and realized that three minutes had passed since her discovery. She pictured herself exploding: her blood splashed on the wispy yellow curtains and soaked into the gray fabric of the dress worn by the woman to her right. Lumps of her heart and brain landed in bowls of the daily special. Her heart beat even faster.

Sandra, once more, checked her watch. Three minutes remained. She could hear her heartbeat. She knew a decision had to be made. She was sure that if she didn't get out of the restaurant she would explode, killing everyone around her. But she was just as convinced that getting up and running would make it real – that her heart would explode only if she gave in to her fear that it would.

She looked at her watch. There was one minute left. She watched the second hand sweep. She stood up. She sat down. She pushed out her chair and took two steps away, and then she ran back to it. She shut her eyes. She grabbed on to the table and ground her teeth together. 'Everybody down!' she shouted, and then nothing happened.

BOOK TWO

7.

On the evening of Wednesday 28th February, seven days after the robbery, there were many reasons not to go to couples counseling: it had been a struggle to get Jasper to bed and we'd just succeeded in doing so; we were both tired, and talking about our marriage, which had not been on solid footings even before the robbery, seemed repetitive and counter-productive. We were weary from two years of looking into his room late at night and being convinced he wasn't breathing, from his not sleeping and our not sleeping and the sleep training. We were drained from the who's-not-carrying-their-weight conversations and the constantly trying to decide whether we were going to have another one or not, and asking ourselves daily if we were good parents and whether we were still in love with each other. But the babysitter was already at the door. So we went.

Our counselor was an elderly woman named Jeanne Roberts, whose long fingers, gray shoulder-length hair, and fleshy ears, which were slightly elongated at the top, gave her a distinctly elfin appearance. Three years ago, when we'd first started seeing her, that she'd looked so much like an elf had been endearing. On several occasions it had greatly contributed to our sticking with it. But on Wednesday 28th February, with Stacey having lost 28 millimeters overnight, 83 millimeters overall, she just seemed stupid.

The three of us sat in her tiny office. I watched Stacey's feet dangle above the carpet. Fifteen minutes into our hour-long session not one of us had spoken.

'Stacey, you look sad today,' Jeanne said, finally. She did not directly mention how much Stacey had shrunk, though it was obvious. Stacey still refused to buy new clothes, so what she wore was many sizes too big.

'Of course I am,' Stacey said.

'Of course,' I repeated.

'David, do you have something you want to say?' asked Jeanne.

'No. Sorry. I'm okay.'

'Doesn't seem like you're okay,' Jeanne said.

'Well, of course she's tired,' I said. There was more anger in my voice than I wanted there to be and I could have left it at that, but I didn't. 'She's always tired. I don't get to be tired.'

'Direct your comments to Stacey, not to me.'

'You're mad because I said I'm tired?'

'She expects everything and gives nothing.'

'Talk to Stacey …'

'I can't believe you're going here.'

'I'm literally carrying you …'

'How long have you been waiting to use that?'

'And you can't even be there when I've had a bad day. I'm not even allowed to have a bad day.'

'David, are you trying to say that you feel underappreciated?'

'That's because every day is a bad day with you. David, you're the reason I'm like this!'

'David?'

I said nothing. I would not look up from the floor.

'I'm the one who's shrinking!' Stacey yelled. 'And all you can do is whine about how hard your life is!'

'So it's my own fault that you've put me at the bottom of your list of priorities?'

'You act like none of this was your decision! The house, the kid – all of it. I need someone who can help me. I need a partner. I need someone who can just be nice to me,' Stacey said.

She said this quietly. She didn't say anything for the rest of the hour, and neither did I.

8.

That night I woke up just after three o'clock in the morning. I don't know what woke me. It wasn't Jasper. I was awake, and in the absence of his screaming I became irrationally angry at him. Of all the nights for him to sleep through, why did it have to be the one that I couldn't? There was only silence, and the silence continued. I looked to my right and Stacey wasn't there.

I pulled the sheets off the bed and I couldn't see her. I lifted the pillow but she wasn't underneath. I got out of the bed and looked under it, fearing that she had already shrunken away to nothing.

I don't know what I'd thought would happen, until then. I may have never really thought it through. I'd imagined she would just keep shrinking, getting smaller and smaller. Maybe we'd have to set up a microscope on the kitchen table or something, but she'd still be around. We'd always have her. She'd just be smaller.

Without getting dressed I rushed out of the bedroom and down the stairs. On the second landing I stopped: I could see her sleeping on the couch. My heart beat quickly. I was out of breath. I didn't know if I should try and get her to come back to bed, so I played it safe and left her. The moment I was back in bed, the phone rang.

'Hello?'

'Oh,' the voice said, 'it's you.'

'Who is this?'

'It's me,' he said, and he did not have to say any more.

'Who do you think you are?' I started. 'You fucking, goddamn—'

'Hey, hey, hey,' he interrupted. His voice was calm and reassuring. 'Listen, maybe you should just, you know, listen, for once. Your wife tells me you're not so good at that.'

'What are you talking about?'

'Calm down. Relax. I'll quit baiting you. Ask me anything you want and I'll answer.'

I did not feel like talking to this thief, and I certainly didn't feel like seeking his wisdom, but what choice did I have?

'Why did you do this?' I asked.

'Because it had to be done.'

'Don't give me that—'

'If you don't like my answer, that's fine. But that is my answer. May we continue?'

'How do we undo it?'

'Do you still love your wife?'

'Of course.'

'Are you sure?' he asked, and there was such permission in his voice. I knew that I could answer no and he wouldn't judge me. That 'no' would be a perfectly acceptable answer here. It made me pause, and within this pause the thief continued.

'Perhaps one of the hardest things about having kids is realizing that you love them more than your wife. That it's possible to love someone more than you love your wife. What's even worse is that it's a love you don't have to work at. It's just there. It just sits there, indestructible, getting stronger and stronger. While the love for your wife, the one you do have to work at, and work so very hard at, gets nothing. Gets neglected, left to fend for itself. Like a houseplant forgotten on a windowsill.'

I didn't know what to say. We were silent for a while.

'Sorry,' the thief finally said. 'I was working up to the houseplant thing. Relying on metaphors too much lately. Anyway, listen, you have no idea how many of these calls I have to make tonight. Take care of yourself. You have quite a fine woman there. Take care of her.'

'Will you call again?' I asked, but the line had already gone dead.

9.

Thirteen days after the robbery, just as the afternoon sun was starting to come in the bedroom window, Stacey was alone in our bedroom, measuring herself without me. She set down the pencil, stepped forward, turned, and looked. Her height was the same as it had been that morning, 1,146 millimeters, a loss of 91 millimeters overnight. She sat down and looked up at the ten black lines on the door jamb, each one marked with the date, her height, and the amount she'd lost overnight.

Stacey stared at the numbers. If I had seen her, I would have told her to stop dwelling on it, to let it go, to focus on the positive. It would never have occurred to me that she was looking for a pattern. Her shrinking seemed such a random and unbelievable thing that I didn't even think to look for some sort of sequence.

Since we hadn't noticed that she was shrinking until three days after the robbery, we didn't know how quickly

41

she shrank on those first days; we only knew that she'd lost 9 millimeters in total. But from that day forward, we'd charted her shrinking on the wall, and these were the numbers Stacey stared at.

'Day 4, 10 millimeters,' she mumbled to herself. 'Day 5, 15 millimeters. Day 6, 21 millimeters.'

The sun had reached our bed. Stacey continued to stare. There did not appear to me to be a sequence. While the numbers were getting larger, they weren't doubling, nor was the rate of shrinking an integer sequence, or some kind of root. The sun was fully in the room, making everything yellow and hopeful, when Stacey suddenly stood up.

'28, 36, 45,' she said. She walked forward and reached up to touch the bottom black line. '55, 66, 78, 91: it's a goddamn triangular number sequence!'

What exactly a triangular number sequence consists of is not an easy concept to grasp. It involves a sequence of equilateral triangles, evenly filled with dots. It is, perhaps, easier to see it.

The sequence starts with 1.

Next is 3.

Add another point to the bottom row, and you have six ...

.
. .
. . .

And then 10 ...

.
. .
. . .
. . . .

and then 15 ...

.
. .
. . .
. . . .
. . . . .

The sequence continues by adding another point to the bottom row of points; the formation remains a stacked series of equilateral triangles. After 15 comes 21, and then 28, 36, 45, 55, 66, 78, 91, 105, 120, 136, 153, 171, 190, 210, 231 ... and so on and so on.

Stacey was invigorated. She'd figured it out. She swayed slightly in the yellow light of the afternoon bedroom sunlight. She was proud of herself for cracking the code, and then, just as quickly, she realized what it meant. She ran out of the bedroom and slid down the stairs. In the kitchen she climbed onto the table and found a pencil and paper. Much later, after all of it was over, I found this scrap of paper, hidden at the back of our closet. The numbers, written in a shaky version of her handwriting, were as follows.

DAY	TALL	LOSS
14	1,146	91
15	1,041	105
16	921	120
17	785	136
18	632	153
19	461	171
20	271	190
21	61	210
22	–	

I can only assume what Stacey did next. I'm almost positive she would have double-checked her calculations. Then she would have reviewed her hypothesis and confirmed it was sound. I imagine her putting down the pencil and sitting. I imagine her beginning to cry. She would have cried and cried. She'd made her shrinking predictable but she'd also proven, beyond a shadow of a doubt, that she would disappear completely in eight days.

This was information she kept from both Jasper and myself. Although Stacey had gone to every meeting of the support group, at this point eight meetings in total, and she'd given me elaborate details about everything that transpired at each one, all the stories of what had happened to whom, that she had discovered the day when she would disappear was something she decided to keep secret.

10.

The only other manifestation that involved shrinking happened to David Bishop, who'd stood first in line and given the thief an old cheap watch. He was driving to his mother's house for dinner when he checked his cell phone and found ninety-eight messages. Every one was from his mother. After listening to the first seventeen, he discovered that the wording in every message was exactly the same. Only her inflection changed with each message, and this only slightly. Pressing some other buttons, he learned that all ninety-eight messages were sent at exactly the same time. He found this strange.

Arriving at his mother's house, he parked and was getting out of the car when he heard a tiny voice. 'Watch out, you oaf,' he heard, barely. Bishop looked down and saw that he was about to step on a very tiny version of his mother, roughly one ninety-eighth her usual size. With his foot hovering in the air he looked at her front yard. It was populated by many tiny versions of his mother. There were tiny mothers on the sidewalk. There were tiny mothers on the porch steps. There were tiny mothers everywhere.

'I'm sorry,' David said. Very carefully he set his foot on the sidewalk.

'Don't be so dramatic,' said a tiny mother. 'It happens with age.'

'No it doesn't.'

'Does too.'

'It hasn't happened to anyone I know.'

'How many old people do you know? It's happened to me.'

'What has?'

'Pick us up. We'll tell you inside,' one of David's tiny mothers said, lifting up her arms. David stooped over and picked her up. As he walked toward the house, every tiny mother lifted her arms in the same fashion. David picked up all of them. Though they were tiny, he could only safely carry twelve at a time. Making nine trips, just to be safe, Bishop collected all ninety-eight of his tiny mothers and set them on the kitchen table in their house. They were slightly smaller then the pepper shaker.

The tiny mothers all looked up at him. Not one of them seemed happy. David couldn't believe how frail his tiny mothers looked. Ninety-eight graying heads, ninety-eight stooped shoulders, one hundred and ninety-six sets of crow's feet around one hundred and ninety-six squinting eyes – in repetition, how she'd aged was impossible to ignore.

He couldn't leave them like this. Carefully he started putting mothers in his pockets. His jacket had six pockets; twelve tiny mothers fitted in each outside pocket, eight in each inside pocket, and twelve tiny mothers fitted in his deep overcoat pockets. Bishop put the remaining thirty-four in the box of a toaster he kept forgetting to return, which had been in his trunk for weeks. Some of the tiny mothers would have preferred outside pockets where they could see, while others would have preferred inside pockets, where it was warmer. None of them wanted to be in the toaster box. Bishop didn't ask their preferences, he just put tiny mothers away as he reached for them. There was a lot of complaining. Carefully he carried the box to the car, carefully setting it on the floor in the back seat. Carefully he got into his car and then he drove home, carefully. Wendy, his wife, was paying bills at the kitchen table when he walked into the house, setting the box beside her.

'I thought you were going to return that,' she said.

Bishop didn't answer her. He started taking tiny mothers out of his pockets and setting them on the dining room table.

'What happened?'

'She seems to have split.'

'Is she staying here?'

'I can't leave her like this.'

'No. I don't suppose you can.'

Although the mothers were tiny, they proved no easier to take care of. Each tiny mother was just as particular in

her eating, sleeping, and social habits as David's mother had been when she'd stood five foot. They all wore the same dress, but had just that one dress to wear. They had no cutlery or plates to eat from, and they were forced to sleep on makeshift beds of Popsicle sticks and cotton wool.

The tiny mothers got all over the house. They would wander away and become unable to find their way back. David was constantly finding tiny mothers hanging from the heating vents or stuck knee-deep in the soil of potted plants. For some reason they especially liked the medicine cabinet. Several went missing.

The next day Wendy called David at work, asking him to come home. When he got there he found more tiny mothers standing on the kitchen table than he could count.

'What's happened?'

'They split again.'

'Really?'

'Yes.'

David watched the tiny mothers split again. Their numbers doubled, as they got doubly small.

'What do we do?' David asked.

'I don't know if there's anything we can do.'

Standing shoulder to shoulder they covered every inch of the dining room table. The tiny mothers split again. Collectively they all raised their heads, motioning David to bend lower. He did, turning his head so his ear was almost touching the tops of their tiny heads.

'We're not afraid,' they said.

'That's good,' David replied. He wanted to hold their hands, but they were so tiny he couldn't even see their hands, so he held Wendy's instead. Moments later the tiny mothers split again and then split once more after that, becoming so small David could only see them if he squinted. Walking to the window, David opened it and let in a breeze that swept across the kitchen table and picked up all the tiny mothers and carried them away.

11.

On Friday 9th March, sixteen days after the robbery, I carried Stacey up the steps of St Matthew's Church. Neither of us knew that this, the twelfth, would be the last meeting of the Branch #117 Support Group. Stacey had gone to each one, watching the attendance dwindle and dwindle.

She was 785 millimeters tall. If you picture the ruler you used all through high school, my wife was one and a half times as long. A list of things taller than my wife would include the seat of her chair, most television sets, and her two-and-a-half-year-old son.

'Jasper, be careful of your mother,' I said. He took a step back and I set Stacey down. She walked inside the church and Jasper reached up and took my hand. I squeezed too hard. Jasper shook his hand free, turned, and hopped down, his feet making a smacking sound as they hit each step. Inside the church, Stacey employed the same technique as she made her way down to the basement.

No folding chairs had been unfolded in the Sunday School room. There were no name tags or Sharpie pens. No smell of brewing coffee. Stacey sat on the bottom step and looked up at the light switch.

The meeting was scheduled to have started fifteen minutes earlier. Stacey was the only one in the room. After twenty more minutes Stacey heard loud commanding steps coming down the stairs. Turning her head, she saw Detective Phillips, whom she hadn't seen since the ninth meeting of the Branch #117 Support Group, and whom she'd simply assumed was dead.

*   *   *

On the day of the robbery, Detective William Phillips had handed the thief a large old-fashioned key, and decided not to play the hero. He was in the bank to pay his phone bill. The key was the original front door key of 152 Patrick Street, in Toronto, Ontario, the house where he'd always lived.

The decision not to play the hero haunted Detective Phillips for the next fourteen days. On the evening of the fifteenth day, shortly after 6.30 p.m, just as he was preparing to leave for the tenth meeting of the Branch #117 Support Group, Detective Phillips was wiping the kitchen table when a large piece of history fell from the ceiling and struck him on the back of the head. He looked up just as the rest of the history became solid and fell.

Two previous generations of Phillipses had lived in the house before him; there was much history to fall. If he had been in the front hallway his chances would have been better. The history there was relatively light, nothing but goodbyes and short-term reunions. But Detective Phillips was in the kitchen, the scene of countless late night desperations and early morning epiphanies, not to mention three conceptions. The most important moments that had happened in the house had occurred in that kitchen. The history that fell was numerous and weighty. It crashed down on Detective Phillips and buried him completely.

'Help!' Detective Phillips called, but no one heard him. The history was piled too high. It covered the windows. It was dark underneath it and hard to move. What little air remained was thick and stifling.

All through the night Detective Phillips repeatedly called out for help, but no help came. He had no food or water. He became weaker and weaker, and obsessed with the thought that none of this would be happening if he'd found the courage to stop the thief. He wouldn't be trapped underneath all of this history. Jenna Jacob and Grace Gainsfield wouldn't have met their unfortunate ends. What was happening to Stacey Hinderland and Dawn Michaels could have been prevented.

Detective Phillips spent the next day trapped beneath his family's history. He spent a second night as well. He slept very little. His hunger and his thirst became over-whelming. In the morning, as he entered his thirty-seventh hour trapped, he grew desperate. Detective Phillips had been afraid to move for fear it would cause the history to shift and crush him. Now he knew he had no other choice, and he began to wiggle and shimmy. The history shifted above him, but instead of taking away the pocket of air he was in, a tiny shaft of light fell upon his eyes. For the first time since being buried alive he could see.

The piece of history in front of him was an inappropriate remark made by a drunken uncle at a tense Christmas dinner. Detective Phillips looked to his right, where his great-grandfather was having a midnight realization that the bills could not be paid. Above that was his great-aunt's tearful confession of repeated extra-marital affairs. With each piece of history Detective Phillips witnessed, he became a little stronger. He wiggled in the history and made enough room to stand. He put his feet on the linoleum floor and pushed and swam upward through the history.

Detective Phillips swam past relatives he'd never met, never even known existed, and watched as they lost their jobs, their spouses, and their hope. He saw failed businesses, broken promises, failed and broken men. In less then six minutes he broke through the top of the pile and swam to the west wall, where he hung onto a curtain rod.

'You're all losers!' he yelled toward the pile of family history. 'We're a family of losers! Three generations of it!' Detective Phillips laughed. He took a very deep breath. He let go of the curtain rod and gracefully dived below the surface.

* * *

As Detective Phillips came down the steps, the musty smell of history preceded him. He stopped three steps above Stacey, shocked by how much smaller she was. He looked around and noticed that none of the chairs were unfolded and that there was no smell of coffee.

'Where is everybody?' he asked.

'I thought I was the only one left,' Stacey said.

'Do you want some help getting up?'

Stacey shook her head no.

'You just want to sit by yourself for a bit?' he asked.

Stacey shook her head yes and then she listened to the sound of his receding steps behind her. She waited for twenty more minutes, but no one else came.

BOOK THREE

12.

Four mornings after the last meeting of the Branch #117 Support Group, Stacey woke up on the couch in the living room with two gigantic eyes staring at her. The eyes were blue and all she could see; the nose was below the cushion, and the forehead was above her field of vision. Stacey became frightened. The eyes continued to stare. They blinked, and then the corners turned upward, and she recognized them as the eyes of her son.

She did not need me to draw a black line on the white paint to know that she'd lost 210 millimeters overnight and that she was now 61 millimeters tall. She was now smaller than a car key.

According to the math, this would be the last morning she'd have with us. Tonight she would not just shrink, but disappear. This was information that I did not have, at the time. She hadn't told me that she'd cracked the code, and that she knew she was about to shrink away.

I still don't know why she didn't tell me.

Stacey was filled with sadness that morning. She looked up at Jasper and saw this sadness in his eyes. Quickly, she sat up and forced herself to smile.

'Good morning, baby!' she screamed.

'Mommy!'

'Wanna do a trick?'

'Ya!' Jasper said. Hopping with both feet together, he rotated clockwise.

'Okay, but you have to be careful with Mommy.'

'Careful with Mommy.'

'Very careful – okay?'

'Careful with Mommy,' Jasper said, nodding. He squished up his face to show that he was concentrating.

'Hold out your finger,' Stacey said. Jasper extended his index finger. 'A little higher, baby. A little higher.'

'Higher,' Jasper repeated. He raised his finger and moved it over the couch. Stacey lifted her hands over her head and grabbed onto it.

'A little lower, baby,' Stacey said. Jasper lowered his finger. Stacey reached around it and locked her fingers together. 'Now, let's go!'

Jasper started to run. Stacey held on tightly. The wind pushed back her hair. Her body swayed to the right and they rounded the corner, into the kitchen. She felt like she was flying and free, but then Jasper came to a sudden stop and the momentum swung her forward. Stacey couldn't keep her grip. She flew through the air, landing awkwardly on the black and white linoleum tiles.

'Stacey!' I yelled. I ran around the kitchen island, stopped in front of her, and leaned down. Jasper began to cry. Stacey sat up and pushed my hands away. She looked at her son.

'Cheerios?' she asked.

'Cheerios!' Jasper yelled, his tears suddenly gone.

I filled an orange plastic bowl with the last of the cereal. Stacey climbed up and onto the table. She tried to hide how heavily she favored her left arm. She took a grape with both hands, closed her eyes, and bit into it.

'Do you have to do that?' I asked.

'Do what?' she asked back, but with all the grape in her mouth, her words came out like: *'Hoo vut?'*

'Hoo vut? Hoo vut?' Jasper said, imitating.

'What if he slipped?'

'Don't overreact.'

'Hoo vut!' Jasper repeated. He hopped up and down on his chair and then lost his footing. His left arm waved as he regained his balance and knocked over the milk, which swept Stacey's feet out from under her.

'I'm okay, I'm okay,' Stacey said, but it was clear that she wasn't. Jasper's cries became screams, which grew louder and louder.

'I'm okay, baby.'

'I'm sorry ...'

'Okay, let's go!' I said. I clapped my hands together. 'Time for school!'

'No!' Jasper said. He repeated this word with increasing vigor as I carried him to the front hallway. 'No. No. No!' he said. I put on his boots and his coat and his hat.

'Just leave him,' Stacey called.

'I'm going to carry you,' I said, as I scooped up my son, 'like a sack of potatoes.'

Jasper laughed. I put him over my shoulder.

'Bye. Bye. Mom. Meey,' Jasper said as he hung over my shoulder. He waved to Stacey in the kitchen. The half-eaten grape was still in her hands. She listened to the front door close, and then suddenly everything was quiet.

13.

That afternoon I stood in aisle six of the Sobey's on Dupont with Stacey inside the breast pocket of my jacket. She could not see out of it. Inside it was dark and stuffy and no matter how carefully I moved, it was impossible for her to keep her balance.

'I don't see them,' I said.

I heard her take a deep breath, and then there was a pause. I'm almost certain she was crying. 'It's the yellow box,' she said, her voice muffled by the fabric.

'Yes. I know it's the yellow box. It isn't there. They must be out of it.'

'They aren't out of Cheerios.'

'Well, it looks like they are.'

'I'm coming up.'

'Hold on,' I told her. At the end of the aisle were two college students buying the breakfast cereals their parents wouldn't let them eat as kids. I waited until they were gone and then I looked to my left. 'Okay,' I said, 'now.'

Several days ago, I'd made a series of cuts into the fabric of my jacket, which led from the bottom of the pocket all the way to my right shoulder. Using these like a ladder, Stacey climbed out of the pocket and reached my shoulder before anyone else came into the aisle.

'For Christ's sake, David,' she said. 'It's right there.'

'Where?'

'There.'

Following the end of her finger I saw the yellow box of Cheerios. 'Oh yes. There they are. Thank you. Do you need help back?' I asked, but by then she'd already returned to the darkness of the pocket.

* * *

While I unloaded the groceries, Stacey climbed over the radio, up the heating vent, and onto the dashboard. Her brow was sweaty, and her tiny chest rapidly rose and fell. I climbed into the driver's seat and shut the door.

'Not safe up there,' I told her. Stacey rolled her eyes. I fastened my seat belt with more force than was necessary.

As we drove out of the parking lot, Stacey sat with her legs in a V, leaning slightly forward with her palms pressed flat against the dashboard to keep her balance. Her hair fell over her face. She swayed slightly to the radio. Traffic was heavy, but it was okay because Stacey looked happy and lighthearted, like she used to look when we'd first started dating. The moment I parked in front of Jasper's daycare she became sad again.

'Why don't you just ride in my pocket?' I asked.

She shook her head and I had to resist the urge to pick her up and carry her with me. Three steps from the car I stopped, sighed deeply, and turned around. Opening the driver's side door, I rolled down the window three inches.

'Sorry,' I said, because she'd already told me that this made her feel like the family dog.

* * *

Stacey sat on the dashboard and took off her shoes and put them back on. She worried that she'd made a horrible mistake – that she should be spending her last hours doing everything she never did, instead of trying to make everything as normal as possible. Her breathing became rapid and shallow. She looked out the window and focused on the gently falling snow, and she regained her calm. Then she saw Dawn running east on College.

Dawn did not look well. Her hair was messy, her shoes untied and her face unwashed. But far more disturbing was how tired she appeared.

Stacey ran along the dashboard, jumped down the steering column and straddled the signal arm. She shimmied to the end of it and used both hands to flash the headlights.

'Dawn!' Stacey yelled. 'In here! In here!'

Stacey's voice was small but it carried out the two inches of open window. Dawn scurried inside the car. She curled into a ball and huddled in front of the driver's seat with her back against the pedals. She looked up at Stacey and then closed her eyes tightly.

The lion rounded the corner. It stopped. Elevating its nose, it sniffed and then walked toward the car.

'Do you see him?' Dawn whispered, her eyes still closed.

'I do,' Stacey replied.

When the lion was parallel with the car, it stopped, raised its head, and sniffed again. It lowered its head and sniffed the concrete. It stepped slowly toward the car. It sniffed the bottom of the door up to the handle.

'Don't move. Don't say a thing,' Stacey whispered.

The lion's claws struck the window. Stacey was knocked forward, and she struggled to regain her balance on the signal arm. She looked up and saw the lion's paws pressed against the glass. Its breath fogged the window in increasingly larger circles.

'Don't let it get in,' Dawn whispered.

Looking down, Stacey saw the keys in the ignition. The lion pounced again, rocking the car. Taking a deep breath, Stacey let herself fall from the signal arm. She fell headfirst, reached out and caught the ring of the key chain as she passed it. She pushed the bright red panic button with her feet; the car's headlights flashed and the horn honked, and then the lion ran away.

After a while, Dawn rose up until her eyes were just above the dashboard. She looked at College Street. She looked left and right and then left again. She turned herself around and slouched into the driver's seat. She held out her hand, which Stacey stepped onto.

'Who's left?' Dawn asked.

'Well,' Stacey said, 'there's me. And there's you.'

'Well, we won't go like Grace Gainsfield,' Dawn said.

'No, we will not go like Grace Gainsfield.'

The two women were silent for several moments.

'I have to go,' Dawn said. She set Stacey on the dashboard and then opened the driver's side door. 'Have to keep moving,' she said. Dawn got out of the car and ran west, and Stacey did not urge her to stay.

14.

Eight days after the robbery, Grace Gainsfield, who had given the thief a small pressed flower that she used as a bookmark, had woken up in cold wet sheets and discovered that her husband had turned into a snowman. Getting out of bed, she stepped in a puddle on the floor. She looked back at her husband. His head was melting faster then the rest of his body; the left side of his face was lopsided, its mouth and eye sockets grotesquely elongated and droopy. The phone rang and, in shock, she answered it.

'Hello?'

'Did I call too early?' her mother-in-law asked.

'No, no. I was up.'

'Can I speak to Daniel?'

'Um. He isn't here.'

'Where is he?'

'Work.'

'At 6.30?'

'You know Daniel.'

'Are you still coming on Thursday?'

'Thursday?'

'For dinner.'

'Oh, yes,' Grace said. 'Absolutely.' She looked down at the floor. The jeans she wore yesterday were at the edge of the puddle, and water had started wicking up the left pant leg. 'Of course we'll be there.'

'Good.'

'I'll have him call you.'

'Thank you. Goodbye then.'

'Bye.'

Grace set the handset back on the cradle. She lifted it up and slammed it back down. She did this three times. She did not look at the bed; she looked at the puddle beneath it. She counted the drops of water falling into it. She noticed that the drops were getting bigger and that the interval between them was rapidly decreasing.

Quickly, without looking at her husband, Grace ran from the room and down the stairs, her wet feet leaving prints on the hardwood floor.

The sun was shining through the large bay window, which made the snowman melt with even greater speed. Grace returned from the kitchen carrying a black plastic garbage bag. She took a deep breath and then slid the bag underneath the snowman. Holding the bag tight, she pulled the snowman off the bed. It landed on the floor with considerable force but remained intact. She pulled it out into the hallway and down the stairs to the basement.

A large white freezer sat against the west wall, humming loudly. Grace emptied it all on the concrete floor. Only then did she realize that the snowman wouldn't fit. Water had already turned the concrete floor a darker gray and begun to pool on the plastic beneath the snowman's head. She ran back up to the kitchen. She collected a large knife, a small paring knife, a roll of paper towels, and the rest of the box of black plastic garbage bags. Carrying these things with her, she ran back down to the basement. She picked up the long knife, twirled it in her hand, and, with great force, severed the snowman's head.

It took several attempts. Her arm was tired before she separated it from the torso. She lifted the head off the black plastic garbage bag and set it inside the freezer.

Changing her grip on the knife, Grace used a stabbing motion to separate the bottom of the snowman from the middle. This she cut into smaller chunks. Ice sprayed everywhere. Her shirt became damp. She hacked the middle until it, too, was in many smaller bits. She placed all of it inside the freezer. Then, gently, she crossed the sticks-for-arms on top of the pieces of the snowman and closed the freezer.

That evening, Grace began to collect snow. She collected snow from the hoods of cars, front porches, and church steps. She collected snow that had been walked on

by many, by none, and only by children. She put out a tray and collected snow that had never touched the ground. She carefully labeled each sample and took it inside, where she held her experiments.

She applied heat and studied the snow as it turned to water. She watched the water turn into vapor. She froze the vapor and studied it as it turned to ice. She worked all night. On Friday she called in sick for work. All day Saturday and all day Sunday she continued to study the snow in all of its states. On Monday she called in sick for work again and continued her experiments.

Just after noon her work was interrupted by a persistent knock on the front door. When she opened it, she saw two detectives, an older one and a younger one. The older one was holding up his badge and spoke first.

'Are you Grace Gainsfield?'

'Yes.'

'May we come in?' asked the younger one.

Grace backed away from her door. She sat at her kitchen table. The detectives stood. 'Are you aware that your husband has been reported missing?' the older one asked.

'No, I wasn't. Thank you.'

'He's been missing for five days now,' said the younger one. 'The report was made by Rebecca Gainsfield. Do you know Rebecca Gainsfield?'

'That's his mother.'

'Yes, it is.'

'It seems a little odd that you weren't the one who reported him missing,' said the younger one.

'Do you know the whereabouts of your husband?'

'Yes. He's in the basement in the freezer,' Grace answered. The detectives exchanged a look.

'Can we see him?'

Grace nodded. She opened the basement door and walked down the stairs. The detectives followed. She opened the freezer. The detectives looked inside. The older one nodded sadly, and the younger one looked at him.

'Okay, thank you, Mrs. Gainsfield,' the older detective said. His voice was gentle and sad. The younger one didn't say anything at all. Leaving the freezer open, Grace showed the detectives to the door.

Grace had many more experiments planned, but she was suddenly quite tired. She made tea but didn't drink it as she sat in their bedroom, looking out the bay window. It began to snow. The snow collected on the windowsill and the tree branches and the sidewalk in front of their house. It seemed unstoppable and infinite. Just as it was getting dark outside, she walked back down to the basement, pulled the freezer from the wall, and tugged the cord from the socket.

The freezer stopped humming. She opened it and climbed inside. She closed the lid.

It was quite cold inside, but the chill eventually dissipated, and the snowman began to melt. The water rose. Soon she could feel it on her shoulders. She closed her eyes as it covered her face.

15.

The construction paper paintings masking-taped to the wall swayed as I walked past them and down the hallway to Jasper's daycare. When he saw me, he did something he'd never done before: he found me more interesting than a percussion instrument. The tambourine fell to the floor as he ran toward me. I opened my arms but he pushed past them, pulled open the breast pocket of my tweed jacket, and looked inside.

'Mommy?' he whispered.

'She's in the car,' I said.

He ran away, picked up the tambourine, and rejoined 'The Wheels on the Bus'. When music class was finished, I helped him into his coat and outside he ran to the car, where he stood in front of the passenger door, jumping up and down.

'Mommy hug, mommy hug, mommy hug,' he screamed.

'Step back, baby,' I said. Jasper continued bouncing. I lifted him up, set him on the sidewalk, and opened the door. He ran and leaped. The upper half of his body landed on the passenger seat but his lower half didn't quite make it. His legs stuck out of the car, his yellow boots kicking in the air, like he was swimming. I looked up to the dashboard to share the scene with Stacey, but she wasn't there.

I picked up Jasper and got several kicks to the chest, but Stacey wasn't beneath him. I put him back on the sidewalk and searched under the passenger seat. I looked under the floor mats, the emergency brake, the pedals. I could not find my wife. On my hands and knees I searched under the passenger seat and the driver's seat. Sippy-cups and toy trains and old newspapers were thrown to the sidewalk. I still couldn't find her. I looked in the back seat and saw her standing on top of the headrest, smiling down at our son while holding her index finger to her lips.

'Jesus Christ, Stacey!' I yelled.

Jasper began to cry. I got out of the car, picked him up and opened the rear door. Stacey climbed down from the headrest and jumped the last couple of inches, landing awkwardly on a seat belt. I swung Jasper into his chair and fought with the straps. Then I stopped, breathed deep, and got down to eye level with him.

'Mommy hug?' I asked.

'Mommy hug!' he squealed. I extended my open palm and Stacey climbed onto it, although we didn't make eye contact, and I lifted her up. Jumping off my hand, she landed on Jasper's chest and climbed up his ski jacket. At the Y formed by the top of the zipper, she raised her arms and grabbed as much of Jasper's throat as she could.

I shut the door and walked around the car. After I'd pulled into traffic, I turned the rearview mirror on a 45-degree angle so I could see both of them. Stacey had climbed up to Jasper's shoulder and was speaking into his ear.

'Played trains!' Jasper said. 'No. No. Mommy no! Pasta!'

'What were you thinking?' I asked her.

'Not now, David.'

'You really thought that was funny?'

'Well, you won't have to put up with me for much longer.'

'What, are you threatening to leave me?'

'You're such an asshole.'

'I'm the asshole?' I asked her. I hit the steering wheel with my fist. Jasper started crying again. I turned in my seat so that I could look at her, and through the passenger window I saw the grill of a minivan quite close and not stopping. It pushed our car sideways through the intersection. I looked up, and then down, and then up again. The sound reminded me of when I lived in Winnipeg, walking on cold crisp snow. Then it was over.

I struggled to turn around but couldn't for a while, until I remembered the seat belt. Unbuckling, I twisted in my seat. Jasper was safely secured in his car seat. The expression on his face asked whether he should be frightened or not. I forced a smile and nodded my head and Jasper laughed. 'Again!' Jasper called, raising his little arms and kicking his little legs. 'Again, Daddy, again!'

Then I saw that she wasn't on his shoulder. 'Stacey?' I called. I leaned into the back seat and searched the floor.

'Stacey?' I repeated. Jasper began crying. There was a knock on the passenger side window. I searched the floor with my hands. His crying became a wail, high-pitched and piercing.

'Hey – are you guys okay?' the other driver asked.

'Stacey?'

'Is that the kid? Is she okay?'

'Stacey!'

'Are you alright?'

'Stacey, where are you?'

I lifted the floor mat and Jasper's screams got louder. The man at the window continued to knock. Then she crawled out from under the seat. There was a cut on her forehead.

'I'm okay, I'm okay,' she said.

'You're hurt.'

'No. Not badly. Just get rid of this idiot.'

I looked out the passenger window and noticed the driver for the first time. 'You almost killed all of us,' I said. 'Go and get your registrations and insurance.'

The man disappeared from the window. I bent back toward the floor and carefully picked up my wife. I held her up so that Jasper could see her.

'Here she is!' I said. 'Here's Mommy.'

'Put me on his shoulder.'

I did as Stacey asked. Jasper stopped crying, but he continued to take long deep breaths. I watched her whisper into his ear.

16.

fter the police and the call to the insurance agent and the tow truck, we were all in the back seat of a taxi heading toward our house. Jasper fell asleep in my arms. Stacey climbed out of my pocket and up to my shoulder. She stood on her tiptoes and kissed the bottom of my earlobe.

'I know things haven't been good for us for a while,' she said. 'But I do love you. I love you and Jasper more than I've ever loved anything in my life.'

Then she sat down and leaned against my neck. The cab continued south on Dufferin. The streetlights shone overhead. Neither of us moved until the taxi stopped in front of our house.

Jasper woke up as I carried him inside. It was past his bedtime but we let him stay up. He played trains on the living room floor, ramming a red one into a blue one in a way that mimicked the crash. I took some cotton from the end of a Q-tip and used Scotch Tape to fasten it over the cut above Stacey's eye. The bleeding stopped but she continued to sit on the living room floor, staring at the wall.

From the hallway I watched both of them, wondering why Stacey couldn't have been one of the people whose manifestation had actually helped their lives.

* * *

George Walterby had stood twelfth in line and given the thief his daughter's pacifier, which he had accidentally put in his pocket that morning. When he got home, he discovered that his baby had begun to shit money: tens, twenties, the occasional hundred.

Over the course of the next three days the baby didn't sleep a lot, but every time they changed her diaper there was money inside. The baby shit enough money that the parents didn't have to worry about money anymore, which was a big relief since that's what they had been worried about, before the robbery.

'We have the perfect baby,' George said.

Then, overnight, the baby got a fever. They took her to the doctor. The doctor shone a light in her eyes. He looked concerned and ordered tests. A machine was attached to the baby's index finger. A nurse drained blood from her tiny arm. George had to look away.

Afterwards, George and his wife settled the baby down and waited with her in an over-lit room with curtains for walls. Children cried all around them. Three hours later the doctor returned. He went straight to the baby and shone the light in her eyes again.

'Have you noticed anything special about her?' the doctor asked.

'She shits money,' George said.

'Hmmm,' the doctor said, and he retreated through the curtain. Two more hours passed and then he returned again.

'She's very sick, and we need to operate,' the doctor said. 'The operation will fix her, but she will cease to excrete currency.'

'Do it,' George and his wife said in unison.

The doctors performed the operation, and the baby got better immediately. They took her home. The baby played and was happy, but George remained worried.

All afternoon he watched his daughter's diaper sag. He did not change her. Just before evening he picked her up and set her on the couch. He pulled open the plastic tabs. He took a very deep breath. He took off her diaper. When all he found inside was shit George became happier than he'd ever been in his life.

* * *

The day after she attended the first meeting of the Branch #117 Support Group and two weeks after her fourth miscarriage, Diane Wagner and her husband had retreated to their cottage when they noticed a storm coming in from the lake. Diane rushed around and closed the window in the living room, and her husband closed the windows in the bathroom and the kitchen. They rushed upstairs and closed all the windows up there. They sat on the bed and listened to the storm, which was directly overhead.

Thump, they heard. *Thump! Thump! Thump!*

'Those are awfully large raindrops,' her husband said.

'Yes,' Diane agreed. She was strangely nervous as she stood and walked to the window. Her palms were sweaty as she unlocked it. Her heart beat wildly as she opened the sash, reached outside and caught one.

17.

I left Stacey and Jasper in the living room and went into the kitchen and put the kettle on the stove, and then the phone rang. This time I heard it – it was an alarm, not a ring, and I raced to answer it.

'Can I speak to Stacey?'

'Who's calling?'

'It's Dawn,' she said. I carried the phone to the living room. Stacey and Jasper were playing trains on the carpet. Setting the bottom end of the receiver in front of her, I pushed the button for speakerphone and went back into the kitchen, where I listened over the sound of the boiling water.

* * *

Dawn had been running from her lion, as she had been for the last eighteen days. Ducking into the liquor store at Bloor and Ossington she was pretty sure that it hadn't seen her. She walked through the wines trying to catch her breath. In the middle of Australian she saw a purple hat on the other side of the aisle.

She followed him to the back of the store, and she was about to confront him when she heard screaming. Turning, she saw the lion bound into the store.

The staff and customers fled. Dawn, the thief, and the lion were alone in the store. Its claws clicked on the floor as it walked toward them. Dawn and the thief stepped backward until they were cornered. The thief pressed his back against the bottles of bourbon and Dawn pressed hers against the rum.

'Do you remember me?' she asked him.

'I do,' he said. 'I presume this is yours?'

Dawn nodded her head. The lion pushed hot breath through its nostrils. Dawn and the thief flinched. Bottles fell off the shelves and broke open as they hit the floor.

'Now would be a good time to let me know how to make it stop.'

Dawn looked at the thief and saw that he was more afraid than she was. She looked at the lion and saw that its gaze was not so much threatening as quizzical. It was the first time she'd been close enough and calm enough to see this. Her fear began to diminish. She clapped her hands once and the lion looked at her. It tilted its head sideways. Dawn extended her finger. She pointed at the thief.

'Get him,' Dawn said.

* * *

'Is he dead?' Stacey asked.

'No. But I let it hurt him. He's in the hospital.'

'Do you think that was okay?'

'I don't know, but as soon as I called it off, it went back to being a tattoo on my leg.'

Stacey looked up from the floor. She touched the makeshift bandage on her forehead.

'Kind of weird,' Dawn continued, but there was no response from Stacey. I heard Dawn repeatedly call her name. I heard Jasper pick up the phone and pretend to have a conversation. I edged up to the kitchen wall and I heard Stacey using the knotted rope we'd run down the stairs so she could climb them on her own.

In the bedroom she scrambled over dress shoes until she'd reached the door jamb. She pushed her bare heels against the white wood. Extending her index finger, the tip of which was now smaller than the point of a pencil, she placed it flat against the top of her head. She touched the wall and closed her eyes. She waited for several moments, and then she waited several moments more. Keeping her finger in place, Stacey turned around to look. The tip of her finger rested directly on that morning's line. She remained 61 millimeters tall.

18.

That evening, Stacey stood in front of Jasper's door for a very long time. He did not cry or moan or even toss his tiny body underneath his covers. Still she continued to stand there. Then she turned and walked away.

'David?' she whispered. 'I have something to tell you.'

'I'm in the bath,' I called.

Stacey came into the bathroom. Candles were lit. I'd also hollowed out a sponge to create something like a pool lounger for her.

'Come in,' I said, and I held out my hand.

I will never know why she agreed to get in. Maybe the emotions the accident had stirred up were still with her. Or maybe the fact that she thought she had just hours left made all the resentment and anger irrelevant. Maybe she was simply cold and the water looked warm. I don't know. But she got undressed and I helped her in.

It took several attempts for Stacey to find her balance on the sponge. If I moved even a little it almost swamped her, so I had to stop moving entirely. We both shut our eyes. The candles flickered. She was just dozing off when she drifted toward me, and the back of her head touched my arm. At first I thought it was a bead of water but when I opened my eyes I discovered it was her.

'At least we both fit in the bath now,' I said.

Stacey laughed. The laugh was neither loud nor long, but it was heartfelt. It was the first time I'd made her laugh since she'd begun to shrink. It was the first time I'd made her laugh in a lot longer than that. She looked up at me and smiled. She closed her eyes and sighed, deeply. Tiny ripples spread outward from the sponge she floated upon.

I thought nothing of them. Nor did Stacey. It would take us months before either of us realized that this was the moment when she imperceptibly, microscopically, but undeniably began to grow.

If you enjoyed *The Tiny Wife* we think you'll like Andrew's new book, *Born Weird*.

Here's how it starts ...

W

THE WEIRDS ACQUIRED THEIR SURNAME through a series of events that some would call coincidence and others would call fate.

Sterling D. Wyird, in the process of emigrating from England to Canada, worked his way across the Atlantic aboard the Icelandic fishing trawler *Örlög*. Inclement weather and empty nets made the six-week journey three months long. When Sterling finally stepped onto the freshly built planks of Pier 21 in Halifax he presented his papers to an immigration guard who, just that morning, had met the woman destined to become his wife. This guard, in a stroke of either inspiration or absent-mindedness, changed the *y* in Sterling's last name to an *e*. Seventy-seven years later, as his great-grandchildren gathered for the final game of their high school football team's season, the spelling mistake remained. They were still Weird.

The four oldest siblings – Richard, nineteen; Lucy, seventeen; Abba, sixteen; and Angie, fourteen – were in the stands, ready to watch Kent, the youngest, play football. Or rather to watch Kent sit on the bench as his teammates played football. Kent was in Grade Nine but he'd skipped Grade Six, so he was only thirteen – yet he'd somehow managed to earn a spot as the third-string quarterback. That Kent had spent the season sitting on the bench didn't bother the Weird siblings in the least. They preferred that he should never make it onto the field. The idea of having to watch him play filled them all with anxiety. Which is why the last game of the season was the first they'd come to see.

They stood in the crowd, feeling awkward. Theirs were the only faces not painted blue and white, the school's colours. Their classmates chanted fight songs that they didn't know the words to. But Kent remained safely on the bench.

Then, with fifty-seven seconds left in the game, the team's star quarterback, Kevin Halleck, received a stunning sack and had to be carried off the field. Mike Bloomfield, the second-string quarterback had just been diagnosed with mononucleosis, and therefore was home. The coach looked at Kent and gave him the nod. Kent ran onto the field for the first time that season. Failing to notice that his shoes were untied.

The home team was losing by a field goal. Or, to put it another way, a touchdown would give them the game. The idea that Kent had been given this chance seemed unbelievable to his brother and sisters. It's not as if the Weird children were outcasts. They were popular. They just weren't A-list. To reach the zenith of teenage popularity, at least at F.E. Madill Secondary School, athletic accomplishment was a non-negotiable prerequisite. The sort of popularity that, should Kent win this game, would instantaneously be transferred on to each of them. Angie was very aware that this was the strange thing about excelling in high school – it made you more normal, not more exceptional. And normalcy was what she craved more than anything else.

But did she yell and cheer for Kent? No, she did not. None of them did. They didn't even call out his name. They were terrified. Not one of them spoke as Kent bent down and tied his shoes. Angie searched the crowd but she couldn't see their mother, father or grandmother. Her parents had gone to the airport, or so she believed, to pick up her grandmother, arriving for her annual month-long Christmas visit. The plan had been for everyone to meet in the parking lot before the game. But her parents and grandmother had never arrived. The thought that they were missing Kent's potential moment of triumph was greatly upsetting to Angie. But then she forgave them, instantly. And as Kent called the play she forgot about them completely.

The teams got into position. The siblings remained silent. The blue and white faces surrounding them cheered their heads off.

'Hut!' Kent called.

The centre flicked the ball into his hands. The clock ticked. Kent went back. He threw a pass. It tumbled through the air and into the stands.

The teams huddled again. Kent clapped his hands. Everyone went into formation. Second down with thirty-six seconds left on the clock. The ball was snapped. Kent faked a pass. Then he handed the football to a running back, who was quickly tackled just behind the line of play. It was a loss of two yards.

Twenty-three seconds were left on the clock, which continued to tick. Last down and last chance. The centre snapped the ball into Kent's hands. His brother and sisters still didn't cheer. They were terrified that Kent was going to drop the football. He took two steps back and then a third. He turned his head to the right and raised the ball but he didn't throw it. Angie glanced at the clock. It ticked down through the number thirteen. When she looked back at Kent, she saw him do a very odd thing: he shut his eyes. They remained closed as he tucked the ball against his chest and began to run.

Their breaths held, Richard, Abba, Lucy and Angie watched Kent as he ran forwards. His head was down. His eyes were still closed. He ran directly into the defensive line. For a moment he disappeared behind opposition uniforms – and then there he was, on the other side.

Less than twenty yards separated Kent and the goal line. At the five-yard line a lanky safety caught up to him. The opposing player leapt into the air. He landed heavily on Kent's back. Kent didn't seem to notice. With the safety's arms wrapped around his waist Kent ran over the goal line and into the end zone.

Kent didn't open his eyes until he heard the roar of the crowd. He saw the cheering fans and his astonished siblings and his overjoyed teammates running towards him. Then he saw his grandmother. She stood at the edge of the field. Her face wordlessly conveyed that something horrible had happened. The ball fell out of Kent's hands just as his teammates reached the end zone. They tried to hoist him on their shoulders. But Kent evaded their grasp. He walked to the sidelines, took off his helmet and approached his grandmother.

And so Kent was the first of the Weirds to learn that everything had changed forever.

Their father was dead.

BOOK ONE:

Blessing + Curse = Blursing

On April 7, 2010, eight and a half years after Kent scored his first and only touchdown, Angie Weird stood in a hallway on the fourth floor of the Vancouver and District General Hospital, eavesdropping on her grandmother as she dictated her epitaph. 'Until you realize that coincidences don't exist, your life will be filled with them,' Grandmother Weird said. 'Everywhere you look there coincidences will be. Coincidence! Coincidence! Coincidence! But the moment you accept there is no such thing, they will disappear forever and you'll never encounter another.'

Angie tried not to vomit. The corridor, in fact the whole hospital, smelled like artificial pine. But her grandmother's ridiculous speech was as nausea-making as the smell of disinfectant. Hearing her grandmother's words reminded Angie of everything she disliked about her family, and why she had avoided all contact with them for years. Even though she'd just flown from New York, five and a half hours in the air with a two-hour stopover in

Toronto, Angie decided to return home. She would never, ever, enter her grandmother's hospital room.

Angie turned away from her grandmother's hospital room and towards the elevator. It was at this exact moment that an orderly was checking his phone as he pushed a cart down the hall. He did not look up until his shoulder struck Angie's. Knocked off balance, Angie was sent stumbling into her grandmother's room.

Each of the four beds in Room 4-206 was occupied by an elderly lady. Grandmother Weird was in the bed closest to the door and Angie's stumble concluded at the foot of it. She looked her grandmother over. Her cheeks were rosy. Her eyes were bright. No tubes were attached to her, not even an intravenous line. In no way did Grandmother Weird appear to be on her deathbed.

'That's an awful lot of text,' said a male voice. It came from the speaker in the telephone.

'Then make the letters small,' Grandmother Weird said. She rolled her eyes. She saw Angie. She looked back at the telephone.

'No name? No date?' the speakerphone voice asked.

'Neither.'

'It'll still be really small.'

'I'll need it in thirteen days,' Grandmother Weird said. She reached out her tiny arm. She jabbed her index finger to the telephone, ending the call. Shuffling her body back into the middle of the bed she looked her granddaughter over.

'Does it have a father?' Grandmother Weird asked.

'Are you asking if this is the child of God?'

'How far along?'

'They looked at me funny in the airport.'

'But no ring …'

'Who am I to go against family tradition?' Angie asked. Grandmother Weird issued a small laugh. She hadn't been married when she'd given birth to her only son, Besnard, Angie's father. The laugh made Angie feel slightly safer. She attempted to sit on the corner of the bed. The mattress sagged. She slid off. She attempted this several more times. Then she noticed the chair in the corner. Pushing it towards the bed, Angie sat down.

'Are you done?'

'Yes.'

'No more wiggling?'

'Nope.'

'Okay then,' Grandmother said. She smoothed the wrinkles from the sheet. 'I'm dying.'

'Again?'

'I will die at 7:39 p.m. on April 20. Not a second later or a moment earlier.'

'Who doesn't love a countdown?'

'Thirteen days from today.'

'Is there something special about that day?'

'It's my birthday. I guess it slipped your memory?'

'Death's not much of a party.'

'I've asked you to come here because there are mistakes I've made. Mistakes I need your help correcting.'

'I plan on living until I'm at least a hundred. Maybe older.'

'Be quiet, Angelika!'

101

Grandmother Weird said these words in what Angie and her siblings called *the Tone*. They each had a pet theory to explain why it was so effective. Kent's was that her voice became all bass. Abba thought it was the way she stressed each word, making them all sound capitalized. Lucy's explanation was that her lung capacity allowed her to push out twice as much air; therefore her words came out twice as strongly. Angie liked all of these, but she felt that only Richard had gotten it right. His explanation was that she stripped all emotion from her voice, leaving only her harsh judgment.

However it worked, it made Angie comply. She sat still. She folded her hands in her lap. Grandmother Weird didn't speak and more than a minute passed.

'You've always been impatient,' Grandmother Weird finally said. 'Do you know that you were born in a hallway?'

'How could I forget?'

'You almost died in that hallway.'

'Yup.'

'With the cord wrapped so tight around your little throat.'

'Crazy,' Angie said. She'd stopped paying attention to her grandmother. The thought of giving birth in a hallway was so terrifying that she'd begun conjuring the scene in her mind, replaying it over and over. This was the way Angie often dealt with events she feared would happen.

'That's why I gave it to you,' Grandmother Weird said.

'Of course.'

'The power to forgive.'

102

'I know. Wait. Gave me what?'

'It was your father's fault. That idiotic car. Whoever heard of driving a Maserati in the city? I knew it would define you.'

'The car?'

'I knew you'd spend your whole life having to find it in yourself to forgive your parents for almost killing you before you were even born. With your very first breath you needed the power to forgive. It's odd because forgiveness is not something I'm particularly good at. I didn't even know I had it in me.'

'What are we talking about?'

'The ability to forgive!'

'...'

'It's my heart,' Grandmother Weird said. 'My goddamn elephant heart.'

Grandmother Weird's heart, while much smaller than an elephant's, *was* unnaturally large. The average human heart weighs between 250 and 350 grams and is about the size of a fist. The weight of Annie Weird's heart pushed 600 grams and it was the size of two fists together. She was convinced that its exaggerated dimensions were the source of all the drama that had ever befallen her. And she was well aware that Angie was her only grandchild who'd inherited this condition. Angie's heart was even slightly bigger than her own.

'I held you in my arms,' Grandmother Weird continued. 'I looked down and it came from me and tumbled into you. I gave to you the power to forgive anyone, anytime.'

Angie looked down at Grandmother Weird. She saw how loosely her rings fit on her fingers, the tremor in her right hand and the droop in her eyelids. 'That's so … it's … it's r … really b … eautiful,' Angie said. She'd started to cry.

'Maybe I should have given you the power not to be such a crybaby sap,' Grandmother Weird said.

Angie had a deserved reputation as the family's crybaby. Yet her grandmother's comment stung. 'Couldn't it have been invisibility?' Angie asked, her tears ceasing, instantly. 'Flight maybe? Something a little more useful?'

'You came out bright red. Not very attractive, I'm afraid. Like a boiled lobster!'

'Super-speed?'

'All of you got one, you know. All five of you got one.'

'You gave Kent the power to be an asshole?'

'Yes. In a way I did. Kent is slightly stronger than anyone he fights. Physical fights, I mean. He came out so small and I knew he'd need to defend himself, somehow. That he's emotionally stunted is not my fault.'

'He's not stunted. He's just angry all the time.'

'Lucy is never lost. Abba never loses hope. Richard keeps himself safe. I never thought they'd all become curses. They were supposed to be blessings. I didn't know that they'd end up ruining your lives.'

'Our lives are ruined?'

'And it's not just you kids. It's the family. The family name! I will not go to the grave responsible for taking down the good name of the Weirds.'

'Oh yes. Well, then, that makes more sense.'

'That's why you're here, Angie. You must go and find them. Round all of them up and bring them here. All five of you must be in this room at 7:39 p.m. on April 20 precisely. At the moment of my death I will lift the curses.'

'Can't you just lift mine now? If it's a curse, the sooner the better, no?'

'Again with the sass! Angie, I have no control over these things. I didn't consciously bestow these abilities. I can't consciously remove them. I just know that at the moment of my death, when my heart is confronted with a now or never situation, it will see the damage these curses have inflicted and take them away.'

'I see,' Angie said. She looked down at her belly. She put both of her hands on the arms of her chair and stood. A blue plastic pitcher sat beside the phone on the bedside table. She filled a Styrofoam cup with water and took a drink.

'Did you hear me?' Grandmother Weird asked.

'Even the water smells like pine.'

'Look at me.'

'Hmmm?'

'You think I've lost my mind.'

'No. Not at all. It's just big. Big news. I just need some time to absorb it, that's all.'

'I see. Perhaps a demonstration then?'

'Not necessary.'

'There' a marker in there,' Grandmother Weird said, pointing to the drawer in the bedside table. 'Could you get it for me?'

Angie opened the drawer. She searched through it. Beneath several celebrity gossip magazines Angie found a black felt-tipped Magic Marker. She handed it over to her. Grandmother Weird took the cap off with her teeth and spit it out, sending it sailing through the air.

The instant the marker hit the floor, every light in the room dimmed by half. The television sets lost reception. Angie felt her grandmother's cold, bony fingers encircle her wrist. She tried to pull away but the old woman's grip was incredibly strong and she could not break it.

'Watch the little old ladies,' Grandmother said.

Angie looked up. The elderly woman closest to the window fell backwards, as if she'd been deboned. The machine beside that bed made a high-pitched whine. Grandmother Weird pressed the Magic Marker against the skin of Angie's forearm and began to write. The lights dimmed further. The white-haired woman in the next bed collapsed. A second machine began making the high-pitched whine. A nurse ran into the room. Angie tried again to pry her grandmother's fingers away. She still couldn't. Grandmother Weird wrote a series of numbers on Angie's skin. The lady in the bed closest fell backwards. A third machine whined. More nurses ran into the room.

'Stop it!' Angie yelled. 'Stop this right now!'

Her grandmother did not look up. She wrote the last number of a ten-digit sequence. Then she let go of Angie's wrist. The lights returned to full-strength. The televisions regained reception. The machines stopped making their high-pitched whines. The elderly women sat upright in their beds and looked around the room, dazed and frightened.

'Never doubt your elders, child.'

'Shark!' Angie yelled. She began to back out of Room 4-206. 'You will never hold my baby. You will never see me again.'

'Yes I will,' Grandmother Weird said. She smiled broadly. She began to laugh. She laughed in *the Tone*.

Angie backed out into the hallway. Holding her belly she ran as fast as she could. She ran towards the elevators. She did not look back. By the time she'd reached them, Angie had already forgiven her grandmother.

NINETY MINUTES AFTER FLEEING her grandmother's hospital room Angie was scrubbing her forearm at a sink in the women's washroom on the departures level of the Vancouver International Airport. She'd rebooked her flight from the back of the taxi she'd taken from the hospital. The only other woman in the bathroom stood at the hand dryer. Her pantsuit was unwrinkled. The diamonds in her ears shone. She pretended not to stare at Angie. Then the dryer shut off and she gave Angie a gentle look as she walked confidently away on her strappy high heels.

Angie looked in the mirror. The front of her white blouse was soaked. Her belly button bulged through the cotton. The ten-digit number remained perfectly legible on her red forearm. When she heard the final boarding call for flight AC117 from Vancouver to New York City, Angie turned off the tap, headed to the gate and boarded the plane.

At row 18 a large man was sitting in the aisle seat. A third of him spilt over the chair. His right arm had already claimed the middle armrest. He did not look up as Angie pushed her purse into the overhead compartment. She stood for several moments before he moved into the aisle and then she wedged herself into the window seat.

Her revenge was how often she had to pee.

Angie made her first trip to the bathroom shortly after takeoff. Her second was twenty minutes later. When she returned from her third visit, the large man had moved to the window.

'Touché,' he said as Angie lowered herself into the aisle seat.

'Thank you,' she replied.

An hour and forty minutes later Angie was in the washroom for the sixth time when the plane began to plummet. She grabbed the faucet with her left hand, cradled her belly with her right and pushed her bum against the door. Water splashed onto the front of her shirt, soaking it once more. She immediately realized that Veronica was a stupid, stupid name. She made a promise to both God and her unborn daughter to find a better one, should they survive.

The dive lasted three long seconds. When the plane levelled off Angie ran back to her seat. She fastened her seat belt, tightly. The large man beside her opened the plastic window shade. They both squinted. When their eyes had adjusted to the light they saw thick black smoke billowing from the plane's far right engine.

'I wouldn't worry. There are three others,' the man sitting beside her said. Then he wiggled into his chair, folded his hands over his chest and closed his eyes.

'Good afternoon,' said an authoritative voice from the speaker over top of Angie's head. 'This is your captain. Yes. We're experiencing some ... minor ... technical difficulties. Nothing to worry about, folks. But we're going to have to make an unscheduled stop. We should be landing in the ... at the ... Winnipeg James Armstrong Richardson International Airport in about fifteen, seventeen minutes. We ... ah ... apologize for the inconvenience. We'll be all right.'

It was the *we'll be all right* that started the panic. There was a collective gasp. Angie's breathing became shallow. Superstition took over and she began to believe that if she could just decide on the perfect name they really would be *all right*. Sarah, Rachael, Jenny, Candi, she thought, desperately. 'Vanessa, Abigail, Helen, Franny,' she said out loud. Then the pressure overwhelmed her imagination and all she could come up with were random nouns. 'Celery, Oboe, Loofah,' she muttered. 'Garamond, Decanter, Frizzante, Pilates. Rolex, Evian, Dasani, Perriella.'

The plane began its descent, which was steep. It dipped forwards. It wobbled to the left and the right. Angie used both of her hands to clutch the armrest as she became convinced that they were all going to die a horrible fiery death.

Then she looked at her forearm and she instantly knew what had to be done. Unfastening her seat belt Angie stepped into the aisle.

'Sit down!' yelled a flight attendant.

'I'm saving us all!' Angie yelled back.

The overhead compartment squeaked as Angie opened it. Pushing back a suitcase that started to fall out, she grabbed her purse, sat back down and fished her phone out. Then Angie dialed the number that she hadn't been able to wash away.

The plane jumped. The phone on the other end began to ring. The runway came into view. 'Hold my hand!' she said to the man beside her. He opened his eyes and looked at Angie, blankly. 'I'm pregnant and alone and frightened and you will hold my goddamn hand!'

Angie held her hand out. Her seatmate took it. He squeezed, tightly. The phone rang for a fourth time. The plane tilted to the right. Several passengers screamed. The phone rang again and then it was answered.

'I'll do it!' Angie yelled. 'I'll get them. I'll get all of them. I'll bring them to you!'

The back tires hit the runway. The plane slowed. The front wheels touched down and the passengers applauded. Angie breathed out. She realized how tightly she was holding both the phone and the hand of the man in the seat beside her.

'I knew you'd come around,' Grandmother Weird said.

'Wait. Wait, wait, wait. Before we commit to anything ...'

'I'd start with Lucy.'

'Well,' Angie said. She looked out the window and then she looked at her hand, which was still engulfed by the meaty palm of her seatmate, 'I *am* in Winnipeg.'

The Tiny Wife is also available as a
specially-priced ebook and audiobook,
available to download from Amazon, Apple
and anywhere else that sells such things.

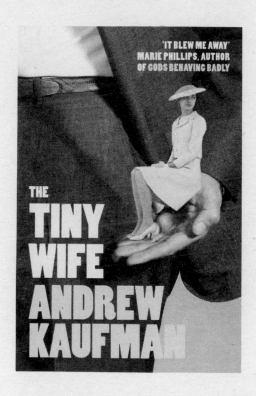